ACADEMY OF DANCE

BFF
BREAKUP

written by
Margaret Gurevich

illustrated by
Claire Almon

STONE ARCH BOOKS
a capstone imprint

Academy of Dance is published by Stone Arch Books,
A Capstone Imprint
1710 Roe Crest Drive
North Mankato, Minnesota 56003
www.capstonepub.com

Library of Congress Cataloging-in-Publication Data
Names: Gurevich, Margaret, author. | Almon, Claire, illustrator.
Title: BFF breakup / by Margaret Gurevich ; illustrated by Claire Almon.
Other titles: Best friend forever breakup
Description: North Mankato, Minnesota : an imprint of Stone Arch Books,
[2018] | Series: Academy of Dance | Summary: When Gabriela hears about
tryouts for a solo dance at the next dance competition she is super excited, but
when Brie, her best friend at Ms. Marianne's Academy of Dance, decides to try
out as well, it seems like it might be the end of a beautiful friendship—because
Gabby really wants this opportunity, and she is having trouble dealing with the
idea of competing against a friend.
Identifiers: LCCN 2018005692| ISBN 9781496562050 (hardcover) |
ISBN 9781496562098 (pbk.)
Subjects: LCSH: Dance—Competitions—Juvenile fiction. | Dance teams—
Juvenile fiction. | Dance schools—Juvenile fiction. | Competition (Psychology)—
Juvenile fiction. | Best friends—Juvenile fiction. | New Jersey—Juvenile fiction.
| CYAC: Dance teams—Fiction. | Competition (Psychology)—Fiction. | Best
friends—Fiction. | Friendship—Fiction. | New Jersey—Fiction.
Classification: LCC PZ7.G98146 Bf 2018 | DDC 813.6 [Fic]—dc23
LC record available at https://lccn.loc.gov/2018005692

Designer: Kay Fraser

Printed and bound in the United States of America.
2411

TABLE OF CONTENTS

CHAPTER 1

A BiG ANNOUNCEMENT

On Saturday afternoon, I walk through
the slush to my favorite place in the world—
Ms. Marianne's Academy of Dance. The small
brick building looks even smaller covered in
snow. But despite the cold, I get that familiar
warm feeling the closer I get.

I open the door and a well-lit hallway greets
me. Studio after studio stretches before me. The
quiet of the New Jersey suburbs disappears as
I'm greeted by the excited voices of the other
girls on my dance team.

On my way to the locker room, I see a group of girls huddled by the wall outside the office, where important announcements are always posted. A familiar red baseball cap catches my eye. It belongs to Brie, my best friend and fellow dance team member.

"Gabby! Over here!" she calls, waving to me.

"What's going on?" I ask, playfully tweaking her cap.

"Solo auditions," Brie whispers.

My heartbeat quickens, and I perk up. I'll take any chance to showcase my jazz moves. Being in front of an audience, shining onstage, is the best feeling in the world. I can already imagine the bright lights and applause.

"For what discipline?" I ask.

Brie shrugs. "The sign just says, *Auditions for Exhibition Performance.* I'm sure Ms. Marianne will tell us more."

As if on cue, Ms. Marianne walks out of the office. She's wearing a purple scarf and leotard, and her salt-and-pepper hair is pulled back into a bun. Her usually serious face breaks into a smile when she sees everyone gathered.

"Ladies," she says, "I'm thrilled so many of you are interested in this opportunity!"

Girls start calling out questions, but it's hard to focus with the millions of questions running through *my* mind. Ms. Marianne claps her hands for silence.

"OK, listen up. There will be an exhibition performance at next month's competition," she explains. "It will allow teams to present a solo of their choosing. We'll be holding auditions in three weeks to determine who will perform the solo. All dance disciplines are welcome. I look forward to witnessing your talent."

The hallway is once again abuzz with excitement.

I overhear Hannah Chang, who's three years older than Brie and me, talking with one of her friends. "Ugh, I just don't know if I have time to practice for a solo," she says.

My heart leaps. Hannah is on both the ballet and tap teams and one of the best dancers at Ms. Marianne's. Brie and I always say we'd like to be as good as she is when we're older. If she doesn't have time to audition, I might actually have a chance at getting the solo.

"Are you going to try out?" I ask Brie. I know what her answer will be, but I ask anyway.

Brie's eyes open wide, and her face flushes. "Are you serious? I get nervous enough before *group* performances. I think I'd faint if I had to dance solo."

I put my arm around my best friend. Brie always panics before performing, but as soon she hits the stage, she's at ease. Brie dances hip-hop, and she's incredibly talented. She reminds me of dancers in music videos.

"If you *did* decide to go for it, people would be scared," I tell her. "Heck, *I'd* be scared. I'm glad to have you rooting for me instead of competing against me."

Brie grins and winks. "Happy to support you from the sidelines."

I hate to admit it, but I'm more relieved than I want to let on. With my best friend out of the running, it's one less person for me to compete against.

CHAPTER 2

JAZZY AND JOYFUL

I spend all weekend thinking about auditions. When Monday's jazz team practice rolls around, the studio is still buzzing with solo talk. Clearly, I'm not the only one with tryouts on the brain.

I give my head a slight shake and remind myself to focus. *There's no chance of you getting a solo if you stop paying attention*, I tell myself firmly.

Our jazz instructor, Ms. Alicia, stands in front of the class, her dark hair pulled back in a bun. "We'll begin with the *pas de bourrée*, back, and turn," she instructs.

I place my right foot behind my left, then put my weight on the ball of my right foot. My left foot glides to the side, and I step on the ball. *Swish.*

My right foot sweeps across the hardwood floor as it finds its place in front again, knee bent. *Swish.* I repeat the same move with my left foot.

"Don't forget arms!" Ms. Alicia calls. She bends her arms, palms down, in front of her chest when her left leg is behind her. When she switches legs, her arms change positions, one to the front and the other to the side.

"And *fondu*," says Ms. Alicia.

I lift my left leg off the ground, placing my left toe just above my right heel, then lower into a *plié.* As I rise back up, I straighten both legs. Nine girls in black leotards, tights, and jazz shoes do the same.

As I study my fellow dancers, the audition poster flashes through my mind. I wonder if anyone else in this group is planning to try out for the solo.

"Pencil turn," says Ms. Alicia.

I smile—I love everything about jazz, but those turns have always been my favorite. I love spinning, whipping my head around to move faster and faster.

I keep my legs pencil straight, my left foot pointed and off the floor. Then I start turning, spotting a corner of the room and coming back to it each time I rotate.

"Again!" exclaims Ms. Alicia.

In unison, we all turn again, looking like music box ballerinas, only faster.

When the class ends, I'm sweaty and tired. My brown hair is falling out of my bun and clinging to my neck and forehead.

But as I walk to the locker room to gather my things, I'm smiling. It's easy to do as I picture myself front and center at the exhibition performance.

CHAPTER 3

FAMILY PRESSURE

"I love going to your house," I tell Brie later that day.

We usually alternate going to each other's houses for dinner after team practices on Saturdays. My family always cooks the Mexican food that Mamá and Abuela grew up eating. Brie's dads are big into barbecue and trying new recipes.

Brie rolls her eyes. "You tell me that every time you come over. I love your family too! You guys have the best food. Plus your *abuela* tells awesome stories, and no one bugs me about 'shining' and 'putting myself out there.'"

I laugh. "Grass is always greener." The thing is, I agree with Brie's dads. She's such a great dancer, but her shyness often stops her from shining even more. It took lots of convincing to even get her to try out for the dance team two years ago.

I grab a handful of Doritos and crumble them over my ice cream. Brie puts her hands to her mouth and pretends to gag.

"Don't knock it until you've tried it," Brie's dad Mike says. He puts ice cream in a bowl and sprinkles Doritos on top. Then he winks at me and shovels a spoonful into his mouth.

"What's going on here?" Brie's other dad, Jeff, asks, joining us at the table. He makes a face at the Doritos and ice cream, then scoops plain vanilla into his bowl and sits beside Brie. "No craziness for us. Right, hon?" He tousles Brie's hair, and she grins.

"What's new in the dance world?" Mike asks.

"Solo auditions!" I blurt out excitedly.

"For everyone?" asks Mike. I can tell he's trying not to sound too hopeful.

"Yup!" I say, digging into my ice cream.

"Could be fun if you two practiced for auditions together," Jeff says, turning to Brie.

Brie's spoon is halfway to her mouth, but she puts it down and frowns. "I don't need to practice since I'm not auditioning. Solos aren't for me. Gabby is super psyched, though. You should talk to her about it."

Mike and Jeff exchange glances. Mike opens his mouth to say something, and Jeff shakes his head. They turn to me.

"So," says Jeff, "when is the audition?"

"Three weeks!" I almost bounce out of my seat. "I have so many moves I need to practice before then!"

I want to say more but peek at Brie. Her bowl is almost empty, but she keeps staring at it and swirling the melted ice cream with her spoon. It's probably best I stop talking about the audition if it's making Brie uncomfortable.

I look at my phone. "It's getting late, and I promised to clean my room. I should probably head home. Thanks for letting me crash dinner."

I give Brie a hug goodbye. I know when I leave, her dads will try to convince her to try out for the solo. As one of her best friends, I will totally support her if she does decide to audition.

But another voice nudges at me too. It reminds me that if Brie tries out, it will be even more competition. It tells me to worry and makes my stomach clench.

Go away! I think. But the voice doesn't fade.

CHAPTER 4

BLINDSIDED

Wednesday afternoon, I'm back at Ms. Marianne's. It's one of my favorite days of the week. Monday, Thursday, and Saturday jazz practices are obviously great. But Wednesdays are mandatory all-team ballet class. That means I get to see my three best friends all in one spot and dance with them for two hours.

"It's Jazz Hands!" my friend Jada calls when I walk into the studio. She splays her fingers wide and waves them in front of her face.

I can't help but laugh. I don't know when *that* became my nickname, but Jada seems to be in a silly mood.

"Uh, OK, Queen Ballerina," I tease back, grinning. Ballet is Jada's number-one focus. Jazz and ballet are actually very similar, but jazz is showier.

Jada laces her fingers together, places them under her chin, and raises her body to her full height. "Queen. I like the sound of that," she says in a fake British accent.

Our friend Grace does a mock bow in Jada's direction. "Your majesty." She swings her arms wide and does one of her signature tap dance moves. It lacks some of her usual pizzazz since she's in her ballet slippers, not tap shoes.

I laugh and move in closer. "Either of you trying out for the solo?" I whisper.

Jada puts her arm around me. "I'm still getting used to things around here. I think I'll pass on adding yet another new thing into the mix."

Jada moved here from Philly over the summer. It was a tough transition at first, but I'm so glad we're all friends now.

"We all take some getting used to," I say with a wink.

"I'll pass too," says Grace. "I have a lot going on at school right now. Plus, I don't think I'll have time to practice for a solo and help my mom with the house." She looks at her toes.

I give Grace a hug. Her parents are divorced, and her dad lives really far away. Everything seems to fall to her and her mom, who works part-time at our dance studio. Grace never complains, though.

"Hey," I say, looking around, "where's Brie?"

As if on cue, Brie comes rushing in. Her face is flushed, and she's trying to yank her hair into a bun as she runs toward us.

"Oh my gosh," she breathes. "We hit the worst traffic. Good thing Ms. Marianne never starts early." She lifts her right leg and places it on the barre for a stretch.

"We were just talking about the solo auditions," says Jada. Her heels touch and her knees bend as she lowers herself from first position to a *plié*.

Brie's cheeks get even redder. She switches legs and turns away from us.

The hair on my arms rises, and I get that weird feeling in my stomach. I focus on pointing my toes to stretch my calves.

Grace looks at Jada and me and raises her eyebrows. "Brie," she says, "are you trying out for the solo?"

Brie lowers her shoulders and slowly faces us. She bites her lip and avoids looking in my direction. "Um, kind of?" she says quietly.

Don't look upset. Don't look upset. Don't look upset, I chant silently. I force a smile. Brie is my friend. I'm supposed to be supportive.

"Wow!" I say with fake enthusiasm. "What made you change your mind?"

Especially since two days ago you didn't even want to talk *about solos*, I think to myself.

Brie sighs. "I really didn't think I wanted to, but the more my dads talked about it, the more I wanted to do it. They convinced me I shouldn't run away from an opportunity. I should challenge myself."

Jada nods. "I totally agree! You're a terrific dancer."

Brie blushes again. "You really think so?"

Grace rolls her eyes. "You know we do!"

They all look at me. My throat is dry. *Am I still smiling?* I wonder.

"Are you mad?" Brie asks.

Maybe? A little? It's just so out of nowhere, I think. I know I need to say something, and it can't be that. "No! Just surprised?"

Brie's face falls. "I didn't mean to blindside you. I was going to tell you. It could be great, right? We can practice together and support each other!" She's talking quickly, like she does when she's trying to convince her dads of something.

Still, she could be right. *This doesn't have to be a competition*, I tell myself. *It's not like we're* both *trying out with a jazz solo.*

I throw my arms around Brie and give her a hug. "Doing this with you will be fun!"

Brie relaxes and smiles. She hugs me back. "Definitely!"

I seem to have convinced everyone I'm fine with Brie auditioning. The problem is, I don't know how to convince *myself.*

CHAPTER 5

BEST FOR WHO?

The next night, I move *frijoles* from one end of my plate to the other. Brie's audition announcement is still on my mind.

"What's wrong, *mija*?" asks Mamá as she places her hand on mine.

"Is it the food?" Abuela worries.

That makes me smile. Abuela shows her love with food. If someone is sad, she thinks a dish, packed with fresh veggies from our garden, can fix it. She doesn't get not being hungry.

"It's *never* your food," I say, giving her a hug. "It's dance."

Mamá's eyebrows furrow. "I thought you loved it."

"I do," I sigh. "More than anything."

Mamá and Abuela exchange confused looks. Abuela stares at my fork. I take a bite to make her feel better. "Brie and I are both trying out for a solo."

"Brie?" Mamá says, surprised.

I nod.

Mamá smiles sympathetically. "I understand it's hard to compete against a friend, but this is good for Brie, isn't it?"

She's on *Brie's* side? "How so?" I ask huffily.

"She's normally so shy. And didn't you tell me she's gotten so nervous that she's gotten sick before competitions before?"

I slump down in my seat. What Mamá is saying is true, so why do I feel like I've been betrayed?

I push my plate away. "Can I finish this later?"

Mamá squeezes my shoulder. "Sure, *mija*." She pats my hand. "Just remember, you and Brie are friends. You want the best for each other."

"Thanks," I mutter, heading up to my room.

I try to ignore the one thought that keeps returning: *At the moment, all I want is what's best for* me.

CHAPTER 6

A NEW SEQUENCE

Normally before dance practice starts on weekdays, I hang out in the hallway and wait for Brie. On Monday, however, I quickly shove my duffel bag into my locker and sprint to the practice studio.

"We're adding a *relevé* and *attitude* turn today," Ms. Alicia says in a singsong voice. Her smile and enthusiasm help push down my negative feelings.

It's all about jazz now, I tell myself. *Nothing else matters.*

Ms. Alicia claps. "Let's take it from the pencil turn!"

I straighten my legs and turn. My eyes immediately find a corner to spot. I finish facing front and straighten my legs before rising onto the balls of my feet for the *relevé.*

"Fantastic!" Ms. Alicia beams. "Now the *attitude* turn."

I move my right foot forward, then cross over with my left. *And lunge*, I think as I bring my right foot forward again, arms spread.

My heart beats quicker as I ready myself for the turn. I push off with my right foot, bring my arms overhead, and bend my left knee behind me. My eyes spot the corner again, and I turn.

I'm focusing on getting my moves right, but I can imagine how great the sequence looks with all of us moving in unison. Ten twirling dancers.

"Bravo!" says Ms. Alicia. "We're going to add a few more combinations, and then we'll take it from the top."

I bite my lip. This is an advanced sequence, and we're not even doing it to tempo yet. *You want that solo, don't you?* I think. *You can do it.*

"From here," Ms. Alicia continues, "I'd like two spiral rolls to the floor."

I feel energy rising from the tips of my toes. I love spirals. Once we get familiar with the whole routine, it will be so worth it.

I lunge forward with my right foot, then move my torso around like a corkscrew. My left knee bends behind me as I land on the floor. Then my knees bend and come together in front of me, and I rise and repeat the move.

"You girls ready to wrap it up?" Ms. Alicia's eyes twinkle.

I look around the room. Everyone's forehead is sweaty. Girls are taking sips from their water bottles. Like me, they seem tired but excited to see how Ms. Alicia will end the routine.

"We'll conclude with two calypso leaps, followed by a pirouette," she tells us. "Got it?"

I nod vigorously. I'll need a breather after that combo, but I can handle it.

"And a one, and a two," Ms. Alicia counts.

I ready myself to take flight. I circle my left arm in front, then point my left leg forward.

"*Chaîné* turn," Ms. Alicia calls. It's a reminder that the calypso leap has other jazz elements too. That's what makes it challenging.

I straighten my arms and put weight on my right foot. Then I move my pointed foot to the side into second position before turning around.

"Excellent!" Ms. Alicia says. "Now downward *chaîné*. Remember to bend those legs."

I repeat my *chaîné* turn, bending low. The next part makes me smile. Keeping my left foot flat on the floor, I point my right foot and swing it around in an arc, like a rainbow, as I jump.

I imagine my foot creating a colorful pattern in the air, all bright and glittery. When I land, I bend my back leg behind me in *attitude.*

"Let's try that again," Ms. Alicia says. "It's one move. Land the rainbow and raise the leg in *attitude* at the same time."

My face flushes. I hate making mistakes.

"And again!" Ms. Alicia instructs.

I repeat the move. This time I land the rainbow and raise my leg in *attitude* at the same time. *Go, me!*

"Almost home, ladies," Ms. Alicia says with a grin. "Pirouette!"

I'm getting winded but push forward. Just one turn to go. I curve my left arm in front of me and move my right out to the side. My left leg bends behind me as I point my toe and lift my heel off the ground.

I sink into a deep *plié* before rising into *relevé* on my right foot. At the same time, I lift my left foot to my right knee.

And spot! My eyes find my favorite corner of the room as I turn, my left foot flying behind me and my arms curved in front of me.

Ms. Alicia claps loudly. "We're running a few minutes over, but let's take a water break, run this from the top, and call it a day. So proud of you all!"

I guzzle my water, feeling strong and confident. If I use this routine in my solo audition, I'm sure to impress Ms. Marianne.

But then I glance out the window that leads to the hallway. Brie is waiting for me, like she does after all team practices. Only this time, my stomach clenches. For the first time since we became friends three years ago, I don't know what to say to her.

CHAPTER 7

Big Fight

"Your jumps and turns are amazing," Brie says as soon as I exit the studio.

I move my hands to the side, wishing leotards had pockets. "Thanks."

Brie seems to sense something is wrong and steps back. "Um, do you want to hang out later? You could come over . . ."

I shrug. "We ended a little late today, and I have homework . . ." My voice trails off.

"Right," Brie says quietly, but she doesn't move to leave. She opens her mouth, then closes it. Saying what's on her mind is hard for her.

"I really do have homework," I say, but I know how lame that sounds. We *always* have homework. It's never stopped us from hanging out before.

Brie shakes her head and swallows. I see her eyes tearing up.

"You're mad at me," she says. "Jada and Grace tried to convince me you were fine with me trying out, but I know you, Gabby. I could *tell* you were mad."

I'm about to deny it, but the feelings I've pushed down bubble up. *Don't*, I tell myself, trying to force them down again. *It's not her fault.*

But I can't help it. I feel tears spring to my eyes too.

"What do you expect, Brie?" I say. "You *never* want to be in the spotlight. *Never.* Then all of a sudden—*after* I tell you how much I want that solo—you decide to audition?"

"I wasn't going to!" Brie says, her voice rising. "But then my dads wouldn't stop talking about how I shouldn't be so scared. They said I should at least try. I *still* didn't want to do it, but I hate always freaking out about being in the spotlight. I thought this would help."

Brie's voice is shaking, and a tear rolls down her cheek. "I thought you'd be proud of me," she continues. "You always side with my dads about stuff like this!"

She's not wrong, but I still can't see this as anything other than her stealing the part from me. "This is different!"

Brie hiccups. "How?"

Suddenly I know. This is the first time Brie's shine could take away *my* sparkle. The thought is awful, and I don't want to voice it.

"It just is!" I shout.

Without waiting for a response, I run to the locker room, grab my duffel bag, and sprint to the parking lot. Tears stream down my face. I picture Brie's face, sad and confused, her feet rooted to her spot in the hallway. It only makes me cry harder.

CHAPTER 8

"You Don't Own Auditions"

"What's wrong with this picture?" Jada asks when she walks into Wednesday's all-team ballet class two days later.

"I don't know what you mean," I say, looking around the room. But I do. Brie is warming up on one end of the barre, and I'm on the other.

Jada rolls her eyes. "Right."

She walks over to Brie, whose smile fades as soon as Jada leans close. Brie shakes her head, and finally turns back to the barre, away from Jada.

Jada stomps back, hands on her hips. "This is ridiculous!"

"What is?" asks Grace.

"These two," says Jada, motioning to Brie and me.

I don't want to hear what either of them has to say and turn away too. I need to practice my calypso leap and pirouette. Hopefully by the time I complete my turn, Jada and Grace will be too busy stretching to lecture me.

No such luck.

"You know," says Grace, lengthening her back to work on her balancing, "you don't own auditions. If my life was less complicated, I'd be trying out too."

I look down at the floor and pretend to focus on pointing my toes.

"If I tried out would we be fighting too, Gabby?" Jada adds.

Ms. Marianne walks in at that moment and saves me from answering. I step away from Jada and Grace. All I want to think about for the next two hours is being the best dancer I can be.

"*Chassé!*" calls Ms. Marianne.

I bring my feet to first position, heels touching. Then I move my heels out to second position, sink into a *plié,* and quickly rise back to first position as I jump. My left foot connects with my right.

"Remember to chase that other foot!" says Ms. Marianne.

Usually that image makes me laugh, but today I glide across the floor without a smile.

"And *jeté!*" Ms. Marianne's voice echoes off the wooden floors.

I *chassé* forward, then leap in the air for my *jeté.* Around me, I hear the soft shuffle of everyone's ballet shoes hitting the floor.

I stay focused on my space. It's all I can
do not to think about Brie or Jada and Grace
dancing nearby.

Beside me, Hannah Chang achieves amazing
height with her *jeté*.

"Beautiful, Hannah," Ms. Marianne
compliments her. Hannah's face is so focused,
I don't think she even hears our instructor's
praise.

"Pirouette, and a one, and a two," Ms.
Marianne says as she taps her thigh.

I focus again. I've been practicing pirouettes
for my jazz routine. I lift my left foot to my
right knee, then swing it behind me as I
turn. I concentrate on pointing my toes and
straightening my leg.

Out of the corner of my eye I see Hannah.
Her pirouettes look effortless. She does three in
a row, followed by a *jeté*.

I'm sure Brie is as awed as I am. I peek behind me and see she's looking my way too. When our eyes meet, she looks away.

Ms. Marianne's instructions float above me, and I try to keep up. But class isn't the same when all your best friends are mad at you.

The problem is I can't figure out why *I'm* so mad at Brie. Grace is right. I don't own auditions. Would I really be as mad at Jada and Grace if they had tried out too? Am I the one being unfair?

CHAPTER 9

Making Things Right

With auditions less than a week away, I spend the rest of the week practicing every chance I get. So does Brie. Not that we're speaking. I only know because I've seen her at the studio.

I've thought of walking up to her and talking things out, but I can't bring myself to do it. Each time I almost get up the guts, my stomach clenches, my palms get sweaty, and I chicken out.

Mamá and Abuela can tell I'm still upset, but other than Abuela making my favorite foods and giving me extra hugs, they've given me space. They both know me well enough to realize there are some things I have to figure out for myself.

That's how I end up on Brie's porch Tuesday after school. I should be practicing for my solo audition, but I can't focus on anything but Brie. I have to talk to my friend.

I take a deep breath and ring the doorbell before I can change my mind. A symphony of chimes sounds inside. I put my ear close to the door to listen for footsteps.

Suddenly the door flies open. Mike beams at me. I thought her dads would be mad at me.

"Hi," I say shyly. "Is Brie home?"

"She's upstairs," Mike says.

When I hesitate, he waves me in and closes the door. I stand in the entryway and bury my hands in the pockets of my jacket. It's warm and toasty in Brie's house, but I pull my jacket tighter around me like I'm trying to hide.

"Go on up," says Mike gently. "I know she'd like to see you."

I came here to make things right, but now I feel paralyzed. "We had a fight," I whisper.

Mike nods. "Friends fight. You two will work it out." He gives me an encouraging smile.

I give him a watery smile back and take a deep breath before heading upstairs. Brie is on her canopy bed reading a magazine. Her door is open, but I knock anyway.

Brie looks up from her magazine, and her eyes grow wide. "Gabs," she says softly.

I walk slowly into her room, afraid she might kick me out.

Maybe Mike was just trying to make me feel better when he said Brie wanted to see me, I think nervously.

"Is that *Just Dance*?" I ask, pointing to the magazine she's holding. It's our favorite, and it makes me sad she's reading the latest issue alone.

"Uh-huh," she says. Brie flips to a new page, but I can tell she's not really reading.

I rub my sweaty palms on my jeans and swallow hard. "I owe you an apology," I begin. "I'm really sorry." I keep my eyes focused on *Just Dance*, afraid of Brie's reaction.

She closes the magazine, and I have no choice but to look at her. Her eyes are a little red, like she's been crying.

"I'm sorry too," she says. "I should have realized you'd be upset."

I put my hand up to stop her. "That's the thing. I had absolutely no right to be upset! I know how hard even *considering* auditioning must have been for you. I should have been supportive."

Brie shakes her head. "But—" she begins.

"I let my fear and jealousy get the best of me," I say. "I was wrong. End of story."

Brie still looks a little unsure. "I should have told you first, not blindsided you like that."

I think about that. Maybe that was one reason I was upset. "I'll give you that one." I tap my lip, thinking. "I guess a part of me felt like you were lying to me when you said you didn't want to try out before."

Brie shakes her head, sending her hair flying around her face. "That wasn't it at all!" she exclaims.

"I know that now," I say. "I probably knew that before too. I just didn't know what to say. Being mad was easier, but it wasn't right. And it definitely wasn't fair to you." I take a seat on Brie's bed.

"I really missed you," Brie says, hugging me.

"Oh my gosh, me too! There are so many things I've been dying to talk about. Like how insane was Hannah's *jeté* at practice last week?"

"Right?" I say. "I knew you'd have something to say about that!"

Brie and I laugh and catch up. We flip through *Just Dance* and try to do the new moves mentioned in the issue. Eventually Brie checks her phone. "Ms. Marianne's is open for another two hours," she says. "Want to go practice for the audition?"

I nervously wait for that weird feeling in the pit of my stomach, but it doesn't come. Instead I feel happy and excited. I *want* to see Brie's hip-hop routine, and I want to show her my jazz combo.

"Let's do it!" I say. I grab her arm, and together we run downstairs.

CHAPTER 10

SOLO TIME

On Saturday afternoon, Brie and I sit outside one of the studios waiting to audition.

"So," Grace says as she and Jada join us, "Jada and I decided we'd give this solo thing a try too."

I roll my eyes. "Super funny."

"Not funny at all," Brie says in mock seriousness. "They're *so* good, they didn't even have to practice."

"You got it," Jada agrees with a wink.

"We're here for moral support," says Grace.

Just then Ms. Marianne opens the studio door. Her eyes meet mine. "Gabby, you're next."

I take a deep breath. "Wish me luck," I say to my friends.

"You'll be great," says Brie, smiling. She raises her hands in the air and wiggles her fingers. "Sending you positive dance vibes."

"Thanks," I murmur as I walk into the dance studio.

Ms. Marianne takes her seat. "I understand you'll be auditioning with your jazz routine?"

I nod and ready myself as the music starts. The *pas de bourrée* is first. I keep one arm curved in front of my chest and the other to the side as my left leg sweeps across the floor. My right foot glides across the hardwood in front of my left. Then I bring my outstretched arm in so both arms curve in front of my chest.

Now the *fondu*. My left toe touches my right heel as I place my weight on one leg and sink toward the floor.

I take a deep breath. The hardest parts of the combination are next.

For the pencil turn, I whirl around, keeping my legs straight. My eyes find a corner to spot. My toes rise in *relevé*, and I turn again, bending my leg behind me in *attitude*.

The music swells around me. All I want to do is move, move, move. My right foot lunges forward, and my torso spirals like a tornado for the spiral roll. I bend my left knee behind me and drop to the floor.

And again, I think as I quickly get up to repeat the move.

I close my eyes and picture the end of the sequence.

My left arm curves in front of me as I point my left leg forward and then to the side in second position. *Whoosh*, I think as I complete my *chaîné* turn.

Now, calypso. I do it again, then swing my right foot around in a rainbow curve. I jump and bend my left leg in *attitude* at the same time, just like Ms. Alicia instructed.

Just a little more, I tell myself. I want this solo so badly, I can taste it.

The pirouette is up next. I bring my right arm to my side, while my left curves in front of me. I quickly spot my corner and touch my left foot to the right knee. My head whips as my left foot swings behind me.

I'm facing Ms. Marianne once again as the music comes to an end. I grin as she applauds.

"That was truly wonderful, Gabby. You should feel very proud."

I take a sip of my water. "Thank you. I do!"

"I'll announce the results tomorrow morning."

I follow Ms. Marianne out of the studio, and my friends jump to greet me.

"How did it go?" asks Jada.

"I'm sure you were amazing," says Brie. I can tell by her voice she really means it.

Ms. Marianne clears her throat. "Sorry to interrupt, ladies, but Brie is next."

"Tell me to break something," says Brie.

I wiggle my fingers in the air, like she did for me. "Positive dancing vibes!"

Brie gives us a small wave before walking into the studio.

My stomach flips nervously, but this time it's not because I don't want Brie to do well. It's because I do, and I'm nervous for her. I close my eyes and wish there was some way for Ms. Marianne to pick two people for solo parts. Because now I want both of us on that stage.

CHAPTER 11

AND THE SOLO GOES TO . . .

As I enter Ms. Marianne's the next day, my phone chimes with a text. *Almost there!* Brie writes. *Wait for me!*

She rushes through the door a few minutes later. A crowd is already gathering by the office, but it doesn't look like anything is posted yet. Finally I see Ms. Marianne walking over.

"Whatever happens, no hard feelings," Brie whispers as we join the other dancers.

"No hard feelings!" I agree. If I don't make it, I hope Brie does. That's what real friendship is. Wanting the best for your friends.

"I want everyone who auditioned to know how impressed I was with your skills," Ms. Marianne starts. "And keep in mind, this was just one opportunity. There will be more."

I can feel the nervous energy. Brie and I bounce on our toes. Girls fidget with their hands.

"I know you're all eager to hear who will be dancing the solo in the exhibition," Ms. Marianne continues.

I rock back on my heels.

"So, I won't keep you in suspense. The solo goes to . . .," says Ms. Marianne.

"I can't take this," Brie mumbles.

"Hannah Chang!" Ms. Marianne announces. "Congratulations!"

We all clap, but my shoulders sag a bit. I see other girls wilt too. But Hannah is beaming.

"Bummer," says Brie.

"I wanted that part so badly," I agree softly.

"Hannah has been dancing longer than us," Brie admits. "She's amazing."

"She's also on *two* dance teams, so she can include both dances in the exhibition," I add.

"She really does deserve this," says Brie.

I nod. "And to think I almost lost you as a friend because of all this!"

Brie shudders. "That would have been awful." Her voice catches. "Pinky swear that will never happen again."

"Never," I say, linking pinkies. "We should go congratulate Hannah."

"Agreed," says Brie.

We link arms and make our way over to Hannah. I still have a competition to look forward to, and I managed to master a difficult new dance routine. But the best part is that whatever happens going forward, I know Brie and I will be there to root for each other.

ABOUT THE AUTHOR

Margaret Gurevich is the author of many books for kids, including Capstone's *Gina's Balance, Aerials and Envy*, and the award-winning Chloe by Design series. She has also written for *National Geographic Kids* and Penguin Young Readers. While Margaret hasn't done performance dance since she was a tween, this series has inspired her to take dance classes again. She lives in New Jersey with her son and husband.

ABOUT THE ILLUSTRATOR

Claire Almon lives and works in Atlanta, Georgia, and holds a BFA in illustration from Ringling College of Art and Design, as well as an MFA in animation from Savannah College of Art and Design. She has worked for clients such as American Greetings, Netflix, and Cartoon Network and has taught character design at Savannah College of Art and Design. Claire specializes in creating fun, dynamic characters and works in a variety of mediums, including watercolor, pen and ink, pastel, and digital.

GLOSSARY

blindsided (BLINDE-sye-did)—unpleasantly surprised

discipline (DIS-uh-plin)—an area of study

enthusiasm (en-THOO-zee-az-uhm)—strong excitement or active interest

exhibition (ek-suh-BISH-uhn)—a public showing, such as for works of art, manufactured goods, or athletic skill

mandatory (MAN-duh-tohr-ee)—required by law or rule

sequence (SEE-kwuhns)—a continuous or connected series

solo (SOH-loh)—an action in which there is only one performer

transition (tran-ZISH-uhn)—a changing from one state, stage, place, or subject to another

unison (YOO-nuh-suhn)—occurring in perfect agreement at the same time

TALK ABOUT IT!

1. Why do you think Gabby reacted the way she did when Brie first announced she was auditioning for the solo? Talk about some possible reasons. Do you think her reaction was fair?

2. Think about the argument Gabby and Brie had from the opposite point of view. Talk about how you would have felt if you were in Brie's shoes.

3. Brie is shy, which makes auditioning for the solo a challenge. Talk about a time you challenged yourself and did something outside your comfort zone. How did it make you feel?

WRITE ABOUT IT!

1. Were you surprised by the outcome of this book? Write a paragraph explaining why or why not. If you were surprised, explain who you expected to get the solo.

2 Pretend you are either Gabby or Brie. Write an apology letter to your friend. Make sure to include both why you were upset and what you did wrong.

3. Have you ever fought with a friend? Write a few paragraphs explaining what your argument was about and how you resolved the conflict.

JAZZ GLOSSARY

Some jazz terms come straight from classical ballet, while others are moves all their own!

attitude (AT-i-tood)—a position in which the dancer stands on one leg; the other leg raised behind the body with the knee bent

ball change (BAHL CHAYNJ)—a change of weight distribution on the balls of the feet. This is a popular transitory step in many jazz dance routines

calypso leap (cah-LIP-soh LEEP)—a turning dance leap in which the working leg is brushed and held straight, while the back leg is held in the attitude position

chaîné (SHIN-neh)—a series of small turning steps. Usually performed on half toe or pointe.

chassé (sha-SEY)—this step resembles a galloping motion, as one foot literally "chases" the other. This is often used in jazz dance terminology to describe a way to travel across the stage, or flow two moves together.

fondu (FAHN doo)—a bending of one's standing leg all the way from relevé to plié

jeté (zhuh-TEY)—a leap in which the dancer propels herself or himself with a push off from one leg, covers space in air, and lands on the other leg

pas de bourrée (PA-duh bur-EY)—a back-side-front three-step move in the floor pattern of an isosceles triangle

pencil turn (PEN-suhl TURN)—a spin done with the non-standing leg pointed toward the floor; the foot hovers off the ground as the dancer turns on the standing leg

pirouette (pir-oo-ET)—a whirling about on one foot or on the points of the toes

plié (plee-EY)—a movement in which the knees are bent while the back is held straight

relevé (REL-uh-vey)—to rise into pointe (on the tips of the toes)

spiral roll (SPY-ruhl ROLL)—a body roll or turn of the body from a standing position that spirals or corkscrews into the floor

THE FUN DOESN'T STOP HERE!

DISCOVER MORE AT
WWW.CAPSTONEKIDS.COM